For Olivia Grace, with love ~ M. C. B.

For my father, Alan R. Macnaughton ~ T. M.

To Emily and Devin
Love,
Grammie + Pa
Feb. 7, 2007

Copyright © 2006 by Good Books, Intercourse, PA 17534
International Standard Book Number: 978-1-56148-532-1; 1-56148-532-2
Library of Congress Catalog Card Number: 2006003269

Text copyright © M. Christina Butler 2006
Illustrations copyright © Tina Macnaughton 2006

Original edition published in English by Little Tiger Press,
an imprint of Magi Publications, London, England, 2006.

Printed in China

Library of Congress Cataloging-in-Publication Data

Butler, M. Christina.
One winter's day / M. Christina Butler ; illustrated by Tina Macnaughton.
p. cm.
Summary: When a wintry wind blows away Little Hedgehog's nest, he sets out
for his friend Badger's house, and the generosity he shows to others during his
journey is returned to him when the snowstorm is over.
ISBN-13: 978-1-56148-532-1 (hardcover)
[1. Hedgehogs--Fiction. 2. Animals--Fiction. 3. Kindness--Fiction. 4. Winter--Fiction.]
I. Macnaughton, Tina, ill. II. Title.

PZ7.B97738One 2006
[E]--dc22
2006003269

One Winter's Day

M. Christina Butler

Illustrated by Tina Macnaughton

Good Books

Intercourse, PA 17534
800/762-7171
www.GoodBks.com

Little Hedgehog was making his bed for the winter when a sudden gust of wind blew him off his feet. It took hold of his cozy nest and tossed it high into the air.

Little Hedgehog trembled as the wind whistled around him, and he wondered what to do.

He caught hold of his scarf, hat and mittens before they blew away, and tried to find shelter under the tree roots. But wherever he went the wind blew there as well.

"I'll have to stay with Badger until this storm has gone," he said at last, pulling his woolly hat firmly over his prickles. Then he snuggled into his cozy scarf, put on his mittens and, with a deep breath, he set off.

The wind was even stronger in the
meadow. Leaves swirled here and there,
and snowflakes filled the air.

Little Hedgehog hadn't gone far when he bumped into a family of field mice shivering in the long grass.

"I've never known such a storm!" squeaked Mother Mouse. "The wind has blown our nest far away, and my poor babies are so cold."

"My home has been blown away as well," said Little Hedgehog. "I'm on my way to stay with Badger, but I have just the thing to warm you up!" And he took off his woolly hat and gave it to the mice.

"Ooh! Lovely, lovely," they squeaked,
snuggling down out of the wind.
"Thank you, Little Hedgehog!"

Little Hedgehog tucked his nose inside his scarf and ran along beside the racing river. Otter was on the bank, huffing and puffing on his paws.

"Hello, Otter!" shouted Little Hedgehog. "What are you doing?"

"Oh hello, Hedgehog," replied Otter. "My fur coat keeps me warm but my paws are freezing!"

"Here, have these," said Little Hedgehog, giving Otter his mittens. "They should do the trick!"

"Thank you, Little Hedgehog!" said Otter. "These are great! But shouldn't you be at home in this cold weather?"

"I have no home anymore," Little Hedgehog replied sadly. "The wind has blown it away." And running on, he cried, "I'm going to stay with Badger!"

By the time Little Hedgehog reached the woods, the snow was getting deeper. On and on he struggled, picking his way between the snowdrifts as the wind howled around him.

A mother deer and her fawn were sheltering in the bushes. "Oh Little Hedgehog, why aren't you in your nest in this awful storm?" she asked.

So Little Hedgehog told Mother Deer about his nest blowing away. But as he spoke he saw that the little fawn was shaking with cold.

"Here, take this," he said, giving the fawn his scarf.

"How kind you are," said Mother Deer. "Thank you, Little Hedgehog."

Little Hedgehog pattered on, faster and faster. But just as he finally saw Badger's house at the bottom of the hill, he skidded on the icy path.

"Help!" he cried as he went bumping and bouncing through the snow.

Badger was making tea when he heard a big THUD! outside. "Whatever was that?" he cried, dropping his toast.

When he opened the door a prickly snowball rolled in. "Gracious me!" he said in surprise. "It's Little Hedgehog!"

Badger carried Little Hedgehog to an armchair by the fire and gave him a cup of tea. Little Hedgehog told Badger about his journey through the storm, and then, cozy and warm, he fell fast asleep.

Little Hedgehog stayed with Badger until the storm had gone. As they walked to where his house had been, Little Hedgehog was very worried. "How can I build a strong new nest if all the leaves and twigs have blown away and there's nothing left?" he asked anxiously. "I'll help you," said Badger kindly. "We're nearly there now."

"Surprise!" came the cry when they turned
the corner. Little Hedgehog gasped with delight.
The animals he'd met in the storm had made
him the coziest nest he'd ever seen.

"For the kindest hedgehog in the world!"
they all cried together.

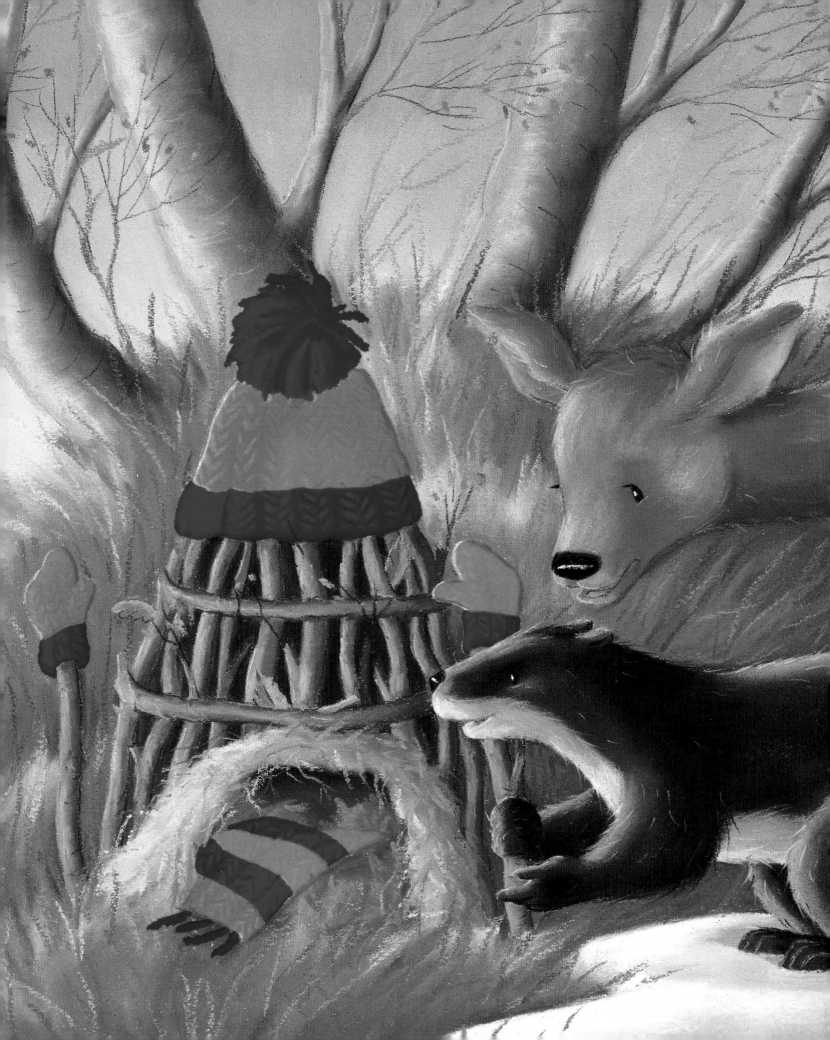